PRIZE SHIP

Prize Ship

by Philip K. Dick

General Thomas Groves gazed glumly up at the battle maps on the wall. The thin black line, the iron ring around Ganymede, was still there. He waited a moment, vaguely hoping, but the line did not go away. At last he turned and made his way out of the chart wing, past the rows of desks.

At the door Major Siller stopped him. "What's wrong, sir? No change in the war?"

"No change."

"What'll we do?"

"Come to terms. Their terms. We can't let it drag on another month. Everybody knows that. *They* know that."

"Licked by a little outfit like Ganymede."

"If only we had more time. But we don't. The ships must be out in deep-space again, right away. If we have to capitulate to get them out, then let's do it. Ganymede!" He spat. "If we could only break them. But by that time—"

"By that time the colonies won't exist."

"We have to get our cradles back in our own hands," Groves said grimly. "Even if it takes capitulation to do it."

"No other way will do*!*"

"You find another way." Groves pushed past Siller, out into the corridor. "And if you find it, let me know."

*

The war had been going on for two Terran months, with no sign of a break. The System Senate's difficult position came from the fact that Ganymede was the jump-off point between the System and its precarious network of colonies at Proxima Centauri. All ships leaving the System for deep-space were launched from the immense space cradles on Ganymede. There were no other cradles. Ganymede had been agreed on as the jump-off point, and the cradles had been constructed there.

The Ganymedeans became rich, hauling freight and supplies in their tubby little ships. Over a period of time more and more Gany ships took to the sky, freighters and cruisers and patrol ships.

One day this odd fleet landed among the space cradles, killed and imprisoned the Terran and Martian guards, and proclaimed that Ganymede and the cradles were their property. If the Senate wanted to use the cradles they paid, and paid plenty. Twenty per cent of all freighted goods turned over to the Gany Emperor, left on the moon. And full Senate representation.

If the Senate fleet tried to take back the cradles by force the cradles would be destroyed. The Ganymedeans had already mined them with H bombs. The Gany fleet surrounded the moon, a little ring of hard steel. If the Senate fleet tried to break through, seize the moon, it would be the end of the cradles. What could the System do?

And at Proxima, the colonies were starving.

"You're certain we can't launch ships into deep-space from regular fields," a Martian Senator asked.

"Only Class-One ships have any chance to reach the colonies," Commander James Carmichel said wearily. "A Class-One ship is ten times the size of a regular intra-system ship. A Class-One ship needs a cradle miles deep. Miles wide. You can't launch a ship that size from a meadow."

There was silence. The great Senate chambers were full, crowded to capacity with representatives from all the nine planets.

"The Proxima colonies won't last another twenty days," Doctor Basset testified. "That means we must get a ship on the way sometime next week. Otherwise, when we do get there we won't find anyone alive."

"When will the new Luna cradles be ready?"

"A month," Carmichel answered.

"No sooner?"

"No."

"Then apparently we'll have to accept Ganymede's terms." The Senate Leader snorted with disgust. "Nine planets and one wretched little moon! How dare they want equal voice with the System members!"

"We could break their ring," Carmichel said, "but they'll destroy the cradles without hesitation if we do."

"If only we could get supplies to the colonies without using space cradles," a Plutonian Senator said.

"That would mean without using Class-One ships."

"And nothing else will reach Proxima?"

"Nothing that we know of."

A Saturnian Senator arose. "Commander, what kind of ships does Ganymede use? They're different from your own?"

"Yes. But no one knows anything about them."

"How are they launched?"

Carmichel shrugged. "The usual way. From fields."

"Do you think—"

"I don't think they're deep-space ships. We're beginning to grasp at straws. There simply is no ship large enough to cross deep-space that doesn't require a space cradle. That's the fact we must accept."

*

The Senate Leader stirred. "A motion is already before the Senate that we accept the proposal of the Ganymedeans and conclude the war. Shall we take the vote, or are there any more questions?"

No one blinked his light.

"Then we'll begin. Mercury. What is the vote of the First Planet?"

"Mercury votes to accept the enemy's terms."

"Venus. What does Venus vote?"

"Venus votes—"

"*Wait!*" Commander Carmichel stood up suddenly. The Senate Leader raised his hand.

"What is it? The Senate is voting."

Carmichel gazed down intently at a foil strip that had been shot to him across the chamber, from the chart wing. "I don't know how important this is, but I think perhaps the Senate should know about it before it votes."

"What is it?"

"I have a message from the first line. A Martian raider has surprised and captured a Gany Research Station, on an asteroid between Mars and Jupiter. A large quantity of Gany equipment has been taken intact." Carmichel looked around the hall. "Including a Gany ship, a new ship, undergoing tests at the Station. The Gany staff was destroyed, but the prize ship is undamaged. The raider is bringing it here so it can be examined by our experts."

A murmur broke through the chamber.

"I put forth a motion that we withhold our decision until the Ganymedean ship has been examined," a Uranian Senator shouted. "Something might come of this!"

"The Ganymedeans have put a lot of energy into designing ships," Carmichel murmured to the Senate Leader. "Their ships are strange. Quite different from ours. Maybe . . . ."

"What is the vote on the motion?" the Senate Leader asked. "Shall we wait until this ship can be examined?"

"Let's wait!" voices cried. "Wait! Let's see."

Carmichel rubbed his jaw thoughtfully. "It's worth a try. But if nothing comes of this we'll have to go ahead and capitulate." He folded up the foil strip. "Anyhow, it's worth looking into. A Gany ship. I wonder . . . ."

*

Prize Ship

Doctor Earl Basset's face was red with excitement.

"Let me by." He pushed through the row of uniformed officers. "Please let me by." Two shiny Lieutenants stepped out of his way and he saw, for the first time, the great globe of steel and rexenoid that was the captured Ganymedean ship.

"Look at it," Major Siller whispered. "Nothing at all like our own ships. What makes it run?"

"No drive jets," Commander Carmichel said. "Only landing jets to set her down. What makes her go?"

The Ganymedean globe rested quietly in the center of the Terran Experimental laboratory, rising up from the circle of men like a great bubble. It was a beautiful ship, glimmering with an even metallic fire, shimmering and radiating a cold light.

"It gives you a strange feeling," General Groves said. Suddenly he caught his breath. "You don't suppose this—this could be a gravity drive ship? The Ganys were supposed to be experimenting with gravity."

"What's that?" Basset said.

"A gravity drive ship would reach its destination without time lapse. The velocity of gravity is infinite. Can't be measured. If this globe is—"

"Nonsense," Carmichel said. "Einstein showed gravity isn't a force but a warpage, a space warpage."

"But couldn't a ship be built using—"

"Gentlemen!" The Senate Leader came quickly into the laboratory, surrounded by his guards. "Is this the ship? This globe?" The officers pulled back and the Senate Leader went gingerly up to the great gleaming side. He touched it.

"It's undamaged," Siller said. "They're translating the control markings so we can use it."

"So this is the Ganymedean ship. Will it help us?"

"We don't know yet," Carmichel said.

"Here come the think-men," Groves said. The hatch of the globe had opened, and two men in white lab uniforms were stepping carefully down, carrying a semantibox.

"What are the results?" the Senate Leader asked.

"We've made the translations. A Terran crew could operate the ship now. All the controls are marked."

"We should make a study of the engines before we try the ship out," Doctor Basset said. "What do we know about it? We don't know what makes it run, or

8

what fuel it uses."

"How long will such a study take?" the Leader asked.

"Several days, at least," Carmichel said.

"That long?"

"There's no telling what we'll run into. We may find a radically new type of drive and fuel. It might even take several weeks to finish the analysis."

The Senate Leader pondered.

"Sir," Carmichel said, "I think we should go ahead and have a test run. We can easily raise a volunteer crew."

"A trial run could begin at once," Groves said. "But we might have to wait weeks for the drive analysis."

"You believe a complete crew would volunteer?"

Carmichel rubbed his hands together. "Don't worry about that. Four men would do it. Three, outside of me."

"Two," General Groves said. "Count me in."

"How about me, sir?" Major Siller asked hopefully.

Doctor Basset pushed up nervously. "Is it all right for a civilian to volunteer? I'm curious as hell about this."

The Senate Leader smiled. "Why not? If you can be of use, go along. So the crew is already here."

The four men grinned at each other.

"Well?" Groves said. "What are we waiting for? Let's get her started!"

*

The linguist traced a meter reading with his finger. "You can see the Gany markings. Next to each we've put the Terran equivalent. There's one hitch, though. We know the Gany word for, say, five. *Zahf.* So where we find *zahf* we mark a five for you. See this dial? Where the arrow's at *nesi?* At zero. See how it's marked?"

```
100   liw
 50   ka
  5   zahf
  0   nesi
  5   zahf
 50   ka
100   liw
```

Carmichel nodded. "So?"

"This is the problem. We don't know what the units refer to. Five, but five what? Fifty, but fifty what? Presumably velocity. Or is it distance? Since no study has been made of the workings of this ship—"

"You can't interpret?"

"How?" The linguist tapped a switch. "Obviously, this throws the drive on. *Mel*—start. You close the switch and it indicates *io*—stop. But how you guide the ship is a different matter. We can't tell you what the meter is for."

Groves touched a wheel. "Doesn't this guide her?"

"It governs the brake rockets, the landing jets. As for the central drive we don't know what it is or how you control it, once you're started. Semantics won't help you. Only experience. We can translate numbers only into numbers."

Groves and Carmichel looked at each other.

"Well?" Groves said. "We may find ourselves lost in space. Or falling into the sun. I saw a ship spiral into the sun, once. Faster and faster, down and down—"

"We're a long way from the sun. And we'll point her out, toward Pluto. We'll get control eventually. You don't want to unvolunteer, do you?"

"Of course not."

"How about the rest of you?" Carmichel said, to Basset and Siller. "You're still coming along?"

"Certainly." Basset was stepping cautiously into his spacesuit. "We're coming."

"Make sure you seal your helmet completely." Carmichel helped him fasten his leggings. "Your shoes, next."

"Commander," Groves said, "they're finishing on the vidscreen. I wanted it installed so we could establish contact. We might need some help getting back."

"Good idea." Carmichel went over, examining the leads from the screen. "Self-contained power unit?"

"For safety's sake. Independent from the ship."

Carmichel sat down before the vidscreen, clicking it on. The local monitor appeared. "Get me the Garrison Station on Mars. Commander Vecchi."

The call locked through. Carmichel began to lace his boots and leggings while he waited. He was lowering his helmet into place when the screen glowed into life. Vecchi's dark features formed, lean-jawed above his scarlet uniform.

"Greetings, Commander Carmichel," he murmured. He glanced curiously at Carmichel's suit. "You are going on a trip, Commander?"

"We may visit you. We're about to take the captured Gany ship up. If everything goes right I hope to set her down at your field, sometime later today."

"We'll have the field cleared and ready for you."

"Better have emergency equipment on hand. We're still unsure of the controls."

"I wish you luck." Vecchi's eyes flickered. "I can see the interior of your ship. What drive is it?"

"We don't know yet. That's the problem."

"I hope you will be able to land, Commander."

"Thanks. So do we." Carmichel broke the connection. Groves and Siller were already dressed. They were helping Basset tighten the screw locks of his earphones.

"We're ready," Groves said. He looked through the port. Outside a circle of officers watched silently.

"Say good-by," Siller said to Basset. "This may be our last minute on Terra."

"Is there really much danger?"

Groves sat down beside Carmichel at the control board. "Ready?" His voice came to Carmichel through his phones.

"Ready." Carmichel reached out his gloved hand, toward the switch marked *mel.* "Here we go. Hold on tight!"

He grasped the switch firmly and pulled.

*

They were falling through space. "Help!" Doctor Basset shouted. He slid across the up-ended floor, crashing against a table. Carmichel and Groves hung on grimly, trying to keep their places at the board.

The globe was spinning and dropping, settling lower and lower through a heavy sheet of rain. Below them, visible through the port, was a vast rolling ocean, an endless expanse of blue water, as far as the eye could see. Siller stared down at it, on his hands and knees, sliding with the globe.

"Commander, where—where should we be?"

"Someplace off Mars. But this can't be Mars!"

Groves flipped the brake rocket switches, one after another. The globe shuddered as the rockets came on, bursting into life around them.

"Easy does it," Carmichel said, craning his neck to see through the port. "Ocean? What the hell—"

The globe leveled off, shooting rapidly above the water, parallel to the surface. Siller got slowly to his feet, hanging onto the railing. He helped Basset up. "Okay, Doc?"

"Thanks." Basset wobbled. His glasses had come off inside his helmet. "Where are we? On Mars already?"

"We're there," Groves said, "but it isn't Mars."

"But I thought we were going to Mars."

"So did the rest of us." Groves decreased the speed of the globe cautiously. "You can see this isn't Mars."

"Then what is it?"

"I don't know. We'll find out, though. Commander, watch the starboard jet. It's overbalancing. Your switch."

Carmichel adjusted. "Where do you think we are? I don't understand it. Are we still on Terra? Or Venus?"

Groves flicked the vidscreen on. "I'll soon find out if we're on Terra." He raised the all-wave control. The screen remained blank. Nothing formed.

"We're not on Terra."

"We're not anywhere in the System." Groves spun the dial. "No response."

"Try the frequency of the big Mars Sender."

Groves adjusted the dial. At the spot where the Mars Sender should have come in there was—nothing. The four men gaped foolishly at the screen. All their lives they had received the familiar sanguine faces of Martian announcers on that wave. Twenty-four hours a day. The most powerful sender in the System. Mars Sender reached all the nine planets, and even out into deep-space. And it was always on the air.

"Lord," Basset said. "We're out of the System."

"We're not in the System," Groves said. "Notice the horizontal curve—This is a small planet we're on. Maybe a moon. But it's no planet or moon I've ever seen before. Not in the System, and not the Proxima area, either."

Carmichel stood up. "The units must be big multiples, all right. We're out of the System, perhaps all the way around the galaxy." He peered out the port at the rolling water.

"I don't see any stars," Basset said.

"Later on we can get a star reading. When we're on the other side, away from the sun."

"Ocean," Siller murmured. "Miles of it. And a good temperature." He removed his helmet cautiously. "Maybe we won't need these after all."

"Better leave them on until we can make an atmosphere check," Groves said. "Isn't there a check tube on this bubble?"

"I don't see any," Carmichel said.

"Well, it doesn't matter. If we—"

"Sir!" Siller exclaimed. "Land."

They ran to the port. Land was rising into view, on the horizon of the planet. A long low strip of land, a coastline. They could see green; the land was fertile.

"I'll turn her a little right," Groves said, sitting down at the board. He adjusted the controls. "How's that?"

"Heading right toward it." Carmichel sat down beside him. "Well, at least we won't drown. I wonder where we are. How will we know? What if the star map can't be equated? We can take a spectroscopic analysis, try to find a known star—"

"We're almost there," Basset said nervously. "You better slow us down, General. We'll crash."

"I'm doing the best I can. Any mountains or peaks?"

"No. It seems quite flat. Like a plain."

The globe dropped lower and lower, slowing down. Green scenery whipped past below them. Far off a row of meager hills came finally into view. The globe was barely skimming, now, as the two pilots fought to bring it to a stop.

"Easy, easy," Groves murmured. "Too fast."

*

All the brakes were firing. The globe was a bedlam of noise, knocked back and forth as the jets fired. Gradually it lost velocity, until it was almost hanging in the sky. Then it sank, like a toy balloon, settling slowly down to the green plain below.

"Cut the rockets!"

The pilots snapped their switches. Abruptly all sound ceased. They looked at each other.

"Any moment . . . " Carmichel murmured:

Plop!

"We're down," Basset said. "We're down."

They unscrewed the hatch cautiously, their helmets tightly in place. Siller held a Boris gun ready, as Groves and Carmichel swung the heavy rexenoid disc back. A blast of warm air rolled into the globe, swelling around them.

"See anything?" Basset said.

"Nothing. Level fields. Some kind of planet." The General stepped down onto the ground. "Tiny plants! Thousands of them. I don't know what kind."

The other men stepped out, their boots sinking into the moist soil. They looked around them.

"Which way?" Siller said. "Toward those hills?"

"Might as well. What a flat planet!" Carmichel strode off, leaving deep tracks behind him. The others followed.

"Harmless looking place," Basset said. He picked a handful of the little plants. "What are they? Some kind of weed." He stuffed them into the pocket of his spacesuit.

"*Stop.*" Siller froze, rigid, his gun raised.

"What is it?"

"Something moved. Through that patch of shrubbery over there."

They waited. Everything was quiet around them. A faint breeze eddied through the surface of green. The sky overhead was a clear, warm blue, with a few faint clouds.

"What did it look like?" Basset said.

"Some insect. Wait." Siller crossed to the patch of plants. He kicked at them. All at once a tiny creature rushed out, scuttling away. Siller fired. The bolt from the Boris gun ignited the ground, a roar of white fire. When the cloud dissipated there was nothing but a seared pit.

"Sorry." Siller lowered the gun shakily.

"It's all right. Better to shoot first, on a strange planet." Groves and Carmichel went on ahead, up a low rise.

"Wait for me," Basset called. He fell behind the others. "I have something in my boot."

"You can catch up." The three went on, leaving the Doctor alone. He sat down on the moist ground, grunting. He began to unlace his boot slowly, carefully.

*

Around him the air was warm. He sighed, relaxing. After a moment he removed his helmet and adjusted his glasses. Smells of plants and flowers were heavy in the air. He took a deep breath, letting it out again slowly. Then he put his helmet back on and finished lacing up his boot.

A tiny man, not six inches high, appeared from a clump of weeds and shot an arrow at him.

Basset stared down. The arrow, a minute splinter of wood, was sticking in the sleeve of his spacesuit. He opened and closed his mouth but no sounds came.

A second arrow glanced off the transparent shield of his helmet. Then a third and a fourth. The tiny man had been joined by companions, one of them on a tiny horse.

"Mother of Heaven!" Basset said.

"What's the matter?" General Groves' voice came in his earphones. "Are you all right, Doctor?"

"Sir, a tiny man just fired an arrow at me."

"Really?"

"There's—there's a whole bunch of them, now."

"Are you out of your mind?"

"No!" Basset scrambled to his feet. A volley of arrows rose up, sticking into his suit, glancing off his helmet. The shrill voices of the tiny men came to his ears, an excited, penetrating sound. "General, please come back here!"

Groves and Siller appeared at the top of the ridge. "Basset, you must be out of—"

They stopped, transfixed. Siller raised the Boris gun, but Groves pushed the muzzle down. "Impossible." He advanced, staring down at the ground. An arrow pinged against his helmet. "Little men. With bows and arrows."

Suddenly the little men turned and fled. They raced off, some on foot, some on horseback, back through the weeds and out the other side.

"There they go," Siller said. "Should we follow them? See where they live?"

"It isn't possible." Groves shook his head. "No planet has yielded tiny human beings like this. So *small!*"

Commander Carmichel strode down the ridge to them. "Did I really see it? You men saw it, too? Tiny figures, racing away?"

Groves pulled an arrow from his suit. "We saw. And felt." He held the arrow close to the plate of his helmet, examining it. "Look—the tip glitters. Metal tipped."

"Did you notice their costumes?" Basset said. "In a storybook I once read. Robin Hood. Little caps, boots."

"A story . . . ." Groves rubbed his jaw, a strange look suddenly glinting in his eyes. "A book."

"What, sir?" Siller said.

"Nothing." Groves came suddenly to life, moving away. "Let's follow them. I want to see their city."

He increased his pace, walking with great strides after the tiny men, who had not got very far off, yet.

"Come on," Siller said. "Before they get away." He and Carmichel and Basset followed behind Groves, catching up with him. The four of them kept pace with the tiny men, who were hurrying away as fast as they could. After a time one of the tiny men stopped, throwing himself down on the ground. The others hesitated, looking back.

"He's tired out," Siller said. "He can't make it."

Shrill squeaks rose. He was being urged on.

"Give him a hand," Basset said. He bent down, picking the tiny figure up. He held him carefully between his gloved fingers, turning him around and around.

"Ouch!" He set him down quickly.

"What is it?" Groves came over.

"He stung me." Basset massaged his thumb.

"Stung you?"

"Stabbed, I mean. With his sword."

"You'll be all right." Groves went on, after the tiny figures.

"Sir," Siller said to Carmichel, "this certainly makes the Ganymede problem seem remote."

"It's a long way off."

"I wonder what their city will be like," Groves said.

"I think I know," Basset said.

"You know? How?"

Basset did not answer. He seemed to be deep in thought, watching the figures on the ground intently.

"Come on," he said. "Let's not lose them."

*

They stood together, none of them speaking. Ahead, down a long slope, lay a miniature city. The tiny figures had fled into it, across a drawbridge. Now the bridge was rising, lifted by almost invisible threads. Even as they watched, the bridge snapped shut.

"Well, Doc?" Siller said. "This what you expected?"

Basset nodded. "Exactly."

The city was walled, built of gray stone. It was surrounded by a little moat. Countless spires rose up, a conglomeration of peaks and gables, tops of buildings. There was furious activity going on inside the city. A cacophony of shrill sounds from countless throats drifted across the moat to the four men, growing louder each moment. At the walls of the city figures appeared, soldiers in armor, peering across the moat at them.

Suddenly the drawbridge quivered. It began to slide down, descending into position. There was a pause. Then—

"Look!" Groves exclaimed. "Here they come."

Siller raised his gun. "My Lord! Look at them!"

A horde of armored men on horseback clattered across the drawbridge, spilling out onto the ground beyond. They came straight toward the four spacesuited men, the sun sparkling against their shields and spears. There were hundreds of them, decked with streamers and banners and pennants of all colors and sizes. An impressive sight, on a small scale.

"Get ready," Carmichel said. "They mean business. Watch your legs." He tightened the bolts of his helmet.

The first wave of horsemen reached Groves, who was standing a little ahead of the others. A ring of warriors surrounded him, little glittering armored and plumed figures, hacking furiously at his ankles with miniature swords.

"Cut it out!" Groves howled, leaping back. "Stop!"

"They're going to give us trouble," Carmichel said.

Siller began to giggle nervously, as arrows flew around him. "Shall I give it to them, sir? One blast from the Boris gun and—"

"No! Don't fire—that's an order." Groves moved back as a phalanx of horses

16

rushed toward him, spears lowered. He swung his leg, spilling them over with his heavy boot. A frantic mass of men and horses struggled to right themselves.

"Back." Basset said. "Those damn archers."

Countless men on foot were rushing from the city with long bows and quivers strapped to their backs. A chaos of shrill sound filled the air.

"He's right," Carmichel said. His leggings had been hacked clean through by determined knights who had dismounted and were swinging again and again, trying to chop him down. "If we're not going to fire we better retreat. They're tough."

Clouds of arrows rained down on them.

"They know how to shoot," Groves admitted. "These men are trained soldiers."

"Watch out." Siller said. "They're trying to get between us. Pick us off one by one." He moved toward Carmichel nervously. "Let's get out of here."

"Hear them?" Carmichel said. "They're mad. They don't like us."

The four men retreated, backing away. Gradually the tiny figures stopped following, pausing to reorganize their lines.

"It's lucky for us we have our suits on," Groves said. "This isn't funny anymore."

Siller bent down and pulled up a clump of weeds. He tossed the clump at the line of knights. They scattered.

"Let's go," Basset said. "Let's leave."

"Leave?"

"Let's get out of here." Basset was pale. "I can't believe it. Must be some kind of hypnosis. Some kind of control of our minds. It can't be real."

Siller caught his arm. "Are you all right? What's the matter?"

Basset's face was contorted strangely. "I can't accept it," he muttered thickly. "Shakes the whole fabric of the universe. All basic beliefs."

"Why? What do you mean?"

Groves put his hand on Basset's shoulder. "Take it easy, Doctor."

"But General—"

"I know what you're thinking. But it can't be. There must be some rational explanation. There has to be."

"A fairy tale," Basset muttered. "A story."

"Coincidence. The story was a social satire, nothing more. A social satire, a work of fiction. It just seems like this place. The resemblance is only—"

"What are you two talking about?" Carmichel said.

"This place." Basset pulled away. "We've got to get out of here. We're caught in a mind web of some sort."

"What's he talking about?" Carmichel looked from Basset to Groves. "Do you know where we are?"

"We can't be there," Basset said.

"*Where?*"

"He made it up. A fairy tale. A child's tale."

"No, a social satire, to be exact," Groves said.

"What are they talking about, sir?" Siller said to Commander Carmichel. "Do you know?"

Carmichel grunted. A slow light dawned in his face. "What?"

"Do you know where we are, sir?"

"Let's get back to the globe," Carmichel said.

*

Groves paced nervously. He stopped by the port, looking out intently, peering into the distance.

"More coming?" Basset said.

"Lots more."

"What are they doing out there *now?*"

"Still working on their tower."

The little people were erecting a tower, a scaffolding up the side of the globe. Hundreds of them were working together, knights, workmen, archers, even women and boys. Horses and oxen pulling tiny carts were drawing supplies from the city. A shrill hubbub penetrated the rexenoid hull of the globe, filtering to the four men inside.

"Well?" Carmichel said. "What'll we do? Go back?"

"I've had enough," Groves said. "All I want now is to go back to Terra."

"Where are we?" Siller demanded, for the tenth time. "Doc, you know. Tell me, damn it! All three of you know. Why won't you say?"

"Because we want to keep our sanity," Basset said, his teeth clenched. "That's why."

"I'd sure like to know," Siller murmured. "If we went over in the corner would you tell me?"

Basset shook his head. "Don't bother me, Major."

"It just can't be," Groves said. "How *could* it be?"

"And if we leave, we'll never know. We'll never be sure. It'll haunt us all our lives. Were we really—*here?* Does this place really exist? And is this place really—"

"There was a second place," Carmichel said abruptly.

"A second place?"

"In the story. A place where the people were big."

Basset nodded. "Yes. It was called—What?"

"Brobdingnag."

"Brobdingnag. Maybe it exists, too."

"Then you really think this is—"

"Doesn't it fit his description?" Basset waved toward the port. "Isn't that what he described? Everything small, tiny soldiers, little walled cities, oxen, horses, knights, kings, pennants. Draw-bridge. Moat. And their damn towers. Always building towers—and shooting arrows."

"Doc," Siller said. "Whose description?"

No answer.

"Could—could you whisper it to me?"

"I don't see how it can be," Carmichel said flatly. "I remember the book, of course. I read it when I was a child, as we all did. Later on I realized it was a satire of the manners of the times. But good Lord, it's either one or the other! Not a real place!"

"Maybe he had a sixth sense. Maybe he really was there. Here. In a vision. Maybe he had a vision. They say that he was supposed to have been psychotic, toward the end."

"Brobdingnag. The other place." Carmichel pondered. "If this exists, maybe that exists. It might tell us . . . . We might know, for sure. Some sort of verification."

"Yes, our theory. Hypothesis. We predict that it should exist, too. Its existence would be a kind of proof."

"The L theory, which predicts the existence of B."

"We've got to be sure," Basset said. "If we go back without being sure, we'll always wonder. When we're fighting the Ganymedeans we'll stop suddenly and wonder—was I really there? Does it really exist? All these years we thought it was just a story. But now—"

Groves walked over to the control board and sat down. He studied the dials intently. Carmichel sat down beside him.

"See this," Groves said, touching the big central meter with his finger. "The reading is up to *liw*, 100. Remember where it was when we started?"

"Of course. At *nesi*. At zero. Why?"

"*Nesi* is neutral position. Our starting position, back on Terra. We've gone the limit one way. Carmichel, Basset is right. We've got to find out. We can't go back to Terra without knowing if this really is . . . . *You know.*"

"You want to throw it back all the way? Not stop at zero? Go on to the other end? To the other *liw?*"

Groves nodded.

"All right." The Commander let his breath out slowly. "I agree with you. I want to know, too. I have to know."

"Doctor Basset." Groves brought the Doctor over to the board. "We're not going back to Terra, not yet. The two of us want to go on."

"On?" Basset's face twitched. "You mean on beyond? To the other side?"

They nodded. There was silence. Outside the globe the pounding and ringing had ceased. The tower had almost reached the level of the port.

"We must know," Groves said.

"I'm for it," Basset said.

"Good," Carmichel said.

"I wish one of you would tell me what it is you're talking about," Siller said plaintively. "Can't you tell me?"

"Then here goes." Groves took hold of the switch. He held it for a moment, sitting silently. "Are we ready?"

"Ready," Basset said.

Groves threw the switch, all the way down.

*

Shapes, enormous and confused.

The globe floundered trying to right itself. Again they were falling, sliding about. The globe was lost in a sea of vague, misty forms, immense dim figures that moved on all sides of them, beyond the port.

Basset stared out, his jaws slack. "What—"

Faster and faster the globe fell. Everything was diffused, unformed. Shapes like shadows drifted and flowed outside, shapes so huge that their outlines were lost.

"Sir!" Siller muttered. "Commander! Hurry! Look!"

Carmichel made his way to the port.

They were in a world of giants. A towering figure walked past them, a torso so large that they could see only a portion of it. There were other shapes, but so vast and dim they could not be identified. All around the globe was a roaring, a deep undercurrent of sound like the waves of a monstrous ocean. An echoing sound, a booming that tossed and bounced the globe around and around.

Groves looked up at Basset and Carmichel.

"Then it's true," Basset said.

"This confirms it."

"I can't believe it," Carmichel said. "But this is the proof we asked for. Here it is—out there."

Outside the globe something was coming closer, coming ponderously toward them. Siller gave a sudden shout, moving back from the port. He grabbed up the Boris gun, his face ashen.

"Groves!" Basset cried. "Throw it to neutral! Quick! We've got to get away."

PHILIP K. DICK

Carmichel pushed Siller's gun down. He grinned fixedly at him. "Sorry. This time it's too small."

A hand was reached toward them, a hand so large that it blotted out the light. Fingers, skin with gaping pores, nails, great tufts of hair. The globe shuddered as the hand closed around them from all sides.

"General! Quick!"

Then it was gone. The pressure ceased, winking out. Beyond the port was—nothing. The dials were in motion again, the pointer rising up toward *nesi*. Toward neutral. Toward Terra.

Basset breathed a sigh of relief. He removed his helmet and mopped his forehead.

"We got away," Groves said. "Just in time."

"A hand," Siller said. "Reaching for us. A big hand. Where were we? Tell me!"

Carmichel sat down beside Groves. They looked silently at each other.

Carmichel grunted. "We mustn't tell anyone. No one. They wouldn't believe us, and anyhow, it would be very damaging if they did. A society can't learn something like this. Too much would totter."

"He must have seen it in a vision. Then he wrote it up as a children's story. He knew he could never put it down as fact."

"Something like that. So it really exists. Both exist. And perhaps others. Wonderland, Oz, Pellucidar, Erewhon, all the fantasies, dreams—"

Groves put his hand on the Commander's arm. "Take it easy. We'll simply tell them the ship didn't work. As far as they're concerned we didn't go anywhere. Right?"

"Right." Already, the vidscreen was sputtering, coming to life. An image was forming. "Right. We won't say anything. Just the four of us will know." He glanced at Siller. "Just the three of us, I mean."

On the vidscreen the image of the Senate Leader was fully formed. "Commander Carmichel! Are you safe? Were you able to land? Mars sent us no report. Is your crew all right?"

Basset peered out the port. "We're hanging about a mile up from the city. Terra City. Dropping slowly down. The sky is full of ships. We don't need help, do we?"

"No," Carmichel said. He began to fire the brake rockets slowly, easing the ship down.

"Someday, when the war is over," Basset said, "I want to ask the Ganymedeans about this. I'd like to find out the whole story."

"Maybe you'll get your chance," Groves said, suddenly sobered. "That's right. Ganymede! Our chance to win the war certainly fizzled."

"The Senate Leader is going to be disappointed," Carmichel said grimly. "You

21

may get your wish very soon, Doctor. The war will probably be over shortly, now that we're back—empty-handed."

*

The slender yellow Ganymedean moved slowly into the room, his robes slithering across the floor after him. He stopped, bowing.

Commander Carmichel nodded stiffly.

"I was told to come here," the Ganymedean lisped softly. "They tell me that some of our property is in this laboratory."

"That's right."

"If there are no objections, we would like to—"

"Go ahead and take it."

"Good. I am glad to see there is no animosity on your part. Now that we are all friends again, I hope that we can work together in harmony, on an equal basis of—"

Carmichel turned abruptly away, walking toward the door. "Your property is this way. Come along."

The Ganymedean followed him into the central lab building. There, resting silently in the center of the vast room, was the globe.

Groves came over. "I see they've come for it."

"Here it is," Carmichel said to the Ganymedean. "Your spaceship. Take it."

"Our time ship, you mean."

Groves and Carmichel jerked. "Your *what?*"

The Ganymedean smiled quietly. "Our time ship." He indicated the globe. "There it is. May I begin moving it onto our transport?"

"Get Basset," Carmichel said. "Quick!"

Groves hurried from the room. A moment later he returned with Doctor Basset.

"Doctor, this Gany is after his property." Carmichel took a deep breath. "His—his time machine."

Basset leaped. "His *what?* His time machine?" His face twitched. Suddenly he backed away. "This? A time machine? Not what we—Not—"

Groves calmed himself with an effort. He addressed the Ganymedean as casually as he could, standing to one side, a little dismayed. "May we ask you a couple of questions before you take your—your time ship?"

"Of course. I will answer as best I can."

"This globe. It—it goes through time? Not space? It's a time machine? Goes into the past? Into the future?"

"That is correct."

"I see. And *nesi* on the dial, that's the present."

"Yes."

"The upward reading is the past?"

"Yes."

"The downward reading is the future, then. One more thing. Just one more. A person going back into the past would find that because of the expansion of the universe—"

The Ganymedean reacted. A smile crossed his face, a subtle, knowing smile. "Then you have tried out the ship?"

Groves nodded.

"You went into the past and found everything much smaller? Reduced in size?"

"That's right—because the universe is expanding! And the future. Everything increased in size. Expanded."

"Yes." The Ganymedean's smile broadened. "It is a shock, is it not? You are astonished to find your world reduced in size, populated by minute beings. But size, of course, is relative. As you discover when you go into the future."

"So that's it." Groves let out his breath. "Well, that's all. You can have your ship."

"Time travel," the Ganymedean said regretfully, "is not a successful undertaking. The past is too small, the future too expanded. We considered this ship a failure."

The Gany touched the globe with his feeler.

"We could not imagine why you wanted it. It was even suggested that you stole the ship to use—" the Gany smiled—"to use to reach your colonies in deep-space. But that would have been *too* amusing. We could not really believe that."

No one said anything.

The Gany made a whistling signal. A work crew came filing in and began to load the globe onto an enormous flat truck.

"So that's it," Groves muttered. "It was Terra all the time. And those people, they were our ancestors."

"About fifteenth century," Basset said. "Or so I'd say by their costumes. Middle Ages."

They looked at each other.

Suddenly Carmichel laughed. "And we thought it was—We thought we were at—"

"I knew it was only a child's story," Basset said.

"A social satire," Groves corrected him.

Silently they watched the Ganymedeans trundle their globe out of the building, onto the waiting cargo ship.

www.ingramcontent.com/pod-product-compliance
Lightning Source LLC
Chambersburg PA
CBHW050921120626
46552CB00004B/1696